Rabbit had a long tail.

But Cat took it as he slept.

"Can I keep it?" she begged,
flicking the long tail.

"Yes," said the unselfish Rabbit,
"if I can have the garden cutters."

“I am happy,” Rabbit grinned.
“I lost a tail but I got the garden cutters.”

As Rabbit hopped along,
he spotted a gardener picking rushes.

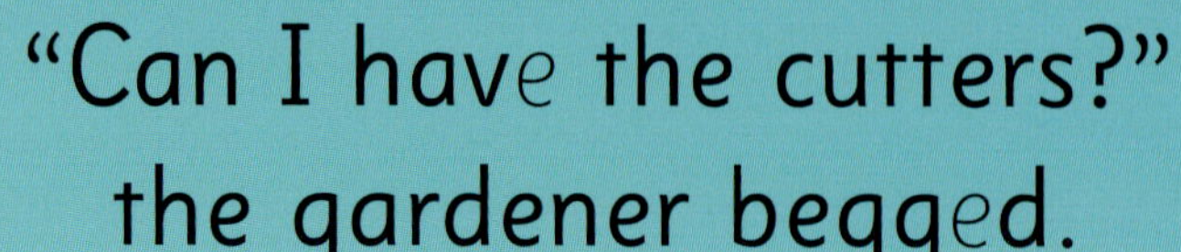

“Can I have the cutters?”
the gardener begged.

“You can keep them,” said Rabbit,
“if I can have a bag.”

The gardener agreed and
handed Rabbit a bag.

“I am lucky,” Rabbit grinned.
“I lost a set of garden cutters
but I got a bag!”

Then, Rabbit spotted a farmer with a load of greens. The farmer dropped the greens onto the ground.

Rabbit handed his bag to the farmer.

“Carry the greens in this,” he said.

The farmer thanked Rabbit
with a big bunch of greens.

From then on, all rabbits have been happy with stumpy tails and greens to munch.